A MESSAGE TO PARENTS

It is of vital importance for parents to read good books to young children in order to aid the child's psychological and intellectual development. At the same time as stimulating the child's imagination and awareness of his environment, it creates a positive relationship between parent and child. The child will gradually increase his basic vocabulary and will soon be able to read books alone.

Brown Watson has published this series of books with these aims in mind. By collecting this inexpensive library, parent and child are provided with hours of pleasurable and profitable reading.

This edition first published 2001 by
Brown Watson, England

Goldilocks
and the Three Bears

Text by Maureen Spurgeon

Brown Watson
ENGLAND

There was once a girl whose hair was so pretty, long, fair and curly, that everyone called her Goldilocks.

Goldilocks and her family lived in a cottage at the edge of a great, big forest, and there was nothing she liked better than going for long walks on her own.

Goldilocks thought she must know every inch of that forest until, one morning, after she had set off a little earlier than usual, she saw something which gave her quite a surprise. . .

It was a little cottage she had never seen before, with lace curtains at the windows and smoke coming out of the chimney. "Who can live here?" wondered Goldilocks, going up to the door.

She knocked at the door and waited. There was no answer. She knocked again. Still, no answer.

"Anyone at home?" she called, and knocked again, a little harder this time. The door creaked open.

Goldilocks stepped inside and
looked all round such a cosy, little
room. A fire burned cheerfully,
and on the hob were three bowls
of porridge - a big bowl, a smaller
bowl, and a tiny, little bowl. . .

"I wonder who lives here?" thought Goldilocks again, never guessing it was the home of three bears - Daddy Bear, Mummy Bear and Baby Bear. She only knew how good that porridge looked on a fresh, spring morning.

She tasted Daddy Bear's porridge. That was too hot. Then, she tried Mummy Bear's porridge. That was too cold. But when she tasted Baby Bear's porridge, it was so good that Goldilocks soon ate it all up!

After eating all that porridge,
Goldilocks wanted to sit down.
So she tried Daddy Bear's chair.
That was too hard. Then she
tried Mummy Bear's chair, but
that was too soft. Then, she tried
Baby Bear's chair. . .

And that was just right! In fact, Goldilocks had never sat in such a comfortable chair! She wriggled and squirmed so much, that, in the end, the chair broke, and Goldilocks fell to the floor!

"Ooh!" she groaned. "I think I'd better go and lie down." So, she went upstairs.

And in the bedroom were three beds - Daddy Bear's bed, Mummy Bear's bed, and Baby Bear's bed. . .

First, she tried Daddy Bear's bed. But that was too hard. Then she tried Mummy Bear's bed. That was too soft. But Baby Bear's bed was so warm and so cosy that Goldilocks snuggled down and was soon fast asleep!

By this time, Daddy Bear, Mummy Bear and Baby Bear were coming back from their walk. They had only gone to the end of the forest path and back - "Just to let the porridge cool down," Mummy Bear had said.

"Who's been eating my porridge?"
growled Daddy Bear.

"Who's been eating my porridge?"
said Mummy Bear.

"Who's been eating my porridge?"
cried Baby Bear. "There's none
left!"

"And who's been sitting in my chair?" roared Daddy Bear.

"Who's been sitting in my chair?" cried Mummy Bear.

"Who's been sitting in my chair?" wailed Baby Bear. "It's all broken!"

They went upstairs. "Who's been sleeping in my bed?" said Daddy Bear.

"Who's been sleeping in my bed?" squealed Mummy Bear.

"Who's been sleeping in my bed?" said Baby Bear, with a loud sob.

His cries woke Goldilocks and she sat straight up in bed. She could not believe her eyes when she saw three furry faces looking at her! "B-bears!" she blurted out, very frightened. "Th-three b-bears!"

Had Goldilocks known it, Daddy, Mummy and Baby Bear were gentle, kind bears. When they saw it was only a little girl who had been in their cottage, they were not nearly so angry as they might have been.

But Goldilocks only knew that she had to leave their cottage just as soon as she could. So she let out a scream, the loudest, longest scream she had ever screamed, making the Three Bears jump back at once!

This was Goldilocks' chance!
She flung back the bedclothes
and rushed out of the door and
down the stairs, away back into
the forest before the Three Bears
knew what was happening!

On and on she ran through the forest until she felt she could run no more.

It seemed a long, long time before she reached the path which led to her own home.

And there was her mother,

waiting anxiously at the gate. Goldilocks was so glad to see her.

"Where have you been, Goldilocks?" she cried. "Daddy was just going out to look for you!"

And so began the story of Goldilocks and the Three Bears. Her mother could hardly believe it!

"You naughty girl!" she scolded. "Haven't I always told you never to go inside strange places?"

"Goldilocks," said her daddy, "are you sure this tale about The Three Bears isn't an excuse because you do not know the forest as well as you thought?"

"No, Daddy!" cried Goldilocks.

"Here," she went on, taking his hand, "I'll take you to their cottage, myself. Then you'll see."

And she led the way back into the forest without stopping once, seeming sure of every step.